ISBN 9780860374916

MUSLIM CHILDREN'S LIBRARY
Miraculous Happenings in "The Year of the Elephant"

Author: Mehded Maryam Sinclair
www.maryamsinclair.com

Illustrator: Ramendranath Sarkar
Cover/Book design & Layout: Nasir Cadir
Coordinator: Anwar Cara

Published by

THE ISLAMIC FOUNDATION
Markfield Conference Centre
Ratby Lane, Markfield
Leicestershire, LE67 9SY, United Kingdom
T: +44 (01530) 244 944 F: +44 (01530) 244 946
E: publications@islamic-foundation.com

Quran House, PO Box 30611, Nairobi, Kenya

PMB 3193, Kano, Nigeria

Distributed by: Kube Publishing Ltd.

British Library Cataloguing in Publication Data

Sinclair, Mehded Maryam
Miraculous happenings in the year of the elephant
1. Legends, Islamic - Juvenile literature
I. Title II. Islamic Foundation (Great Britain)
297.1'8

ISBN-13: 9780860374916

Printed by Proost International Book Production, Belgium

Miraculous Happenings in The Year of the Elephant

MEHDED MARYAM SINCLAIR

ON a steamy-hot day in the Yemen of old a hundred slaves dressed in nothing but tattered rags wrapped around their waists heaved and hauled, hammered and hewed tons of marble and stone for their master, the vice-regent Abrahah.

They worked inside an enormous cloud of rising white dust, dust that clung to their skins, piled up in the hollows of their ears, ringed their eyes and settled in their hair and their beards. They scurried here and there, lugging marble slabs, grinding them into shape for corners and stairs, sanding them smooth. The ring of mallets on chisels stabbed the air; now and then one of them coughed or sneezed the dust out of his nose.

The lean, mean Abrahah came in his swirling black robes and towered over them to inspect, like a black ant wandering amid a pile of sugar cubes. He came only long enough to gloat, and then returned to his chamber of thick carpets and clean air.

Back in the quiet of his chamber, he brushed a bit of the chalky marble dust from his robe and pored over the drawings of the new cathedral. He examined bits of ebony-wood and ivory.

"Yes, these will do…use them for the pulpits and benches in the main chamber."

He closed a deal for the purchase of great marble slabs salvaged from one of the palaces of the Queen of Sheba.

"In the whole wide world there's not a single building as great as this," he boasted. "When the word gets out, pilgrims will come here instead of to Makkah. Why make a pilgrimage to that silly pile of stones they call the Ka'ba?"

His bony hand closed around a goblet of wine and he drank long and greedily. "And when they come, they'll buy and sell, and I will get even richer from all their trade! The Quraysh of the Hollow will fly away like a leaf in the wind. Their city will be deserted, the Ka'ba will melt back into the sand and be forgotten."

Abrahah flung himself down on his brocade sofa and stuffed a handful of black grapes into his mouth. "Bring me Unays, the elephant trainer!"

The year was 570 C.E. and the year had a name. It was
"The Year of the Elephant." It was later in that year
that the Prophet Muhammad would be born, may
Allah bless him and give him peace, to bring News
    of the infinite,
    of that which lasts forever,
    of that from which we came,
    of that which we will know when we die,
to bring this News into ears and into hearts,
to be carried there until the end of time.

Everything was ready for the coming of Islam. The blessed lost waters of Zam Zam were gushing up again out of the dry sands near the Ka'ba. The Jews and the few Christians in Makkah were studying their scriptures and watching for signs of the new prophet who was to come. The parents who would bring him into the world had just gotten married. From near and far pilgrims crowded to Makkah to be near the Ka'ba, the house of Allah since the olden days of the Prophet Ibrahim, peace be upon him.

A little while later, Unays stood before Abrahah with his whip in his hand.

"We need your most powerful elephant! We will march on the Ka'ba and destroy it," shouted the vice-regent.

"At once, Master! My elephant is waiting to serve you."
Unays ran off to prepare his prize elephant, the love of his life.

Everywhere there rose the sounds of preparations. Stable-hands groomed and loaded hundreds of horses. A massive wooden wagon for carrying the elephant loomed up outside the stables. The men hitched five charging horses to it, snapping their whip and shouting out instructions.

Servants were running hither and thither packing up the tent, packing up the carpets, packing up the pots and pans and sacks of rice and ropes of onions, all the things they would need to keep their master comfortable on his journey.

The soldiers said goodbye to their families. They mounted their horses. They stood in long lines to wait for the signal to move. When that shrill sound came, they set off to the north across the desert and the day rolled along under their feet. The news about all of this raced to the ears of the fierce and brilliant Nufayl, the leader of the tribe of Khath'am.

"They will never destroy the Ka'ba," he raged. "It is the house of Allah! It has been standing for eons. It was built by the Prophet Ibrahim, peace be upon him, in a place that had been known to be sacred since time out of mind."

He called up his tribesmen with their weapons. They gathered, armed to the teeth, all along the road that runs between Makkah and the Yemen and waited, determined to stop Abrahah's army.

Alas, Abrahah's army was bigger. The tribesmen were outnumbered seven-to-one. They had to flee for their lives. But Nufayl would not flee, and Abrahah captured him.

Nufayl was smart. And he would do anything to protect the Ka'ba. So he thought of a plan to stop Abrahah's army. He told Abrahah, "Don't kill me yet! I know all these lands between here and Makkah like the back of my hand. If you don't have a good guide, you could end up lost in the desert. Let me guide you."

Abrahah wasn't so smart, and he agreed. His powerful henchmen led Nufayl to the big creaking elephant wagon and bound him hand and foot inside it. The troops pressed ever onward towards their goal.

They came within two miles of Makkah to Mughammis. The servants pitched the vice-regent's magnificent red tent and rolled out the lush carpets inside it. They unpacked the bundles of pots and pans and provisions. They slaughtered a fat goat and roasted it over a fire for Abrahah and his closest advisors. But they had to be content with dates and water.

"Bring me ten of the fastest horses and their riders!" Abrahah barked. The stable boys brought the horses and the ten men came and stood to attention.

"Take a message to the people of Makkah. Tell them that we have come to destroy the Ka'ba. If they don't want their blood to spill, let them send their leader here to me at once!"

The riders mounted their horses and galloped off. The sands swirled around them as they sped along into the desert. They met a caravan heading towards them, on its way to Yemen. They attacked it and plundered it. They sent the money and goods back to Abrahah in his camp. They sent back gold and silver. They sent back silks. They sent back flocks of sheep and goats, sacks of chickens, and the two hundred camels of Abd al Muttalib.

When they rode into Makkah, one of them shouted, "Where is the leader of your city?"

The people of this city, the Quraysh of the Hollow, were the men Allah had appointed to take care of His pilgrims, to give them water and food and places to sleep. They were led by Abd al Muttalib, the one who had found the long-lost waters of Zam Zam; the one who would be the grandfather of the new prophet who was even then waiting in the wings to be born; and the one whose camels had been taken by Abrahah's army.

Everyone knew Abd al Muttalib and loved him. He was noble and kind, courageous and generous. He was one of the few people at that time who could not be satisfied bowing down before statues of wood and stone. He wanted more. He wanted to bow down before the One that had created him and the trees and mountains from which the statues had been made.

Perhaps Allah wanted to show the world something before Islam came into it. Perhaps He wanted people to know for sure that those who rely on Him are victorious. Perhaps He wanted everyone to see that if He says "Be!" it surely is.

Abd al Muttalib pulled aside the curtain of his house and watched the ten riders fill his yard. Their leader spoke from his horse.

"Abrahah, the vice-regent of Yemen, says that if you want to save your life and the lives of your people, you must come at once to see him. He is camped along the way between here and the Yemen."

Abd al Muttalib went with his sons straight out into the desert to Abrahah's encampment.

Now, Abd al Muttalib was a tall and handsome man. He believed in Allah and relied on Him. This made him seem even bigger than he was. When the guards showed him in to Abrahah, the vice-regent's eyes opened wide and he stood up to greet his visitor. The guards looked at each other, surprised. They had never ever seen him stand up to greet anyone before, except his master, the Negus.

Abrahah actually invited Abd al Muttalib to sit down on his carpets.

"Welcome," he said. "You received the message, I presume?"

"Yes," replied Abd al Muttalib.

"Well, what do you have to say?"

"Your army," said Abd al Muttalib, "has taken two hundred of my camels, and I want them back."

"What!" exclaimed Abrahah. "We are here to destroy your holy place, and you are worried about your camels?"

"Well, you see, I am the lord of my camels, but the Ka'ba has a Lord too, and He will defend it."

"Ha! He cannot defend it against me!" shouted Abrahah.

"We shall see. But in any case, give me my camels."

"Guards! Return the camels to this simpleton, and then get him out of here!"

Abd al Muttalib returned to Makkah, driving his camels before him. The men of the city were waiting for him.

"Their army is fierce," he told them. "Take your families and go up into the hills and stay there until we send for you."

Then he went with his sons to the Ka'ba to pray. He took the great ring of the door in his hands and called out, "Oh Allah. Your slave has protected his house, now You protect Yours."

The voices of women and children reached them. Everyone was leaving the city, leading their donkeys loaded with food and bedding. Abd al Muttalib and his sons joined the last group and wound their way through the rocky dry land into the hills. Here, among the crags and cliffs, they hid, looking down on Abrahah's soldiers and horses amassed on the flat ground not far from the House of Allah. The soldiers were awaiting the order of their leader Abrahah to march on it and destroy it.

Abd al Muttalib and his people watched from afar as Unays the elephant trainer led his magnificent animal out of the wagon and paraded him in front of the commanders and soldiers and horses. The elephant was hung with bright carpets and colourful ribbons. His trainer turned him so he was facing the Ka'ba and then stood near him waiting for the order to begin the attack.

21

But the eyes of Unays were turned away from his prize animal. He was busy looking at Abrahah so he could see the signal to begin.

Nufayl was there too. His feet had been unbound, but he still had his hands tied behind his back and nobody noticed him. He'd had plenty of time in the last few days to watch the trainer and his elephant. By the will of Allah, he had learned all the commands that the elephant knew.

Now, while everybody was watching Abrahah for the signal to move, Nufayl crept quietly up to the elephant on the right side. He bent his head towards the massive ear and said, in a deep quiet voice, "KNEEL!"

The great beast bent first one front knee and then the other and settled his front half on the ground. Nufayl slipped away before anyone could see him. Then the elephant's hind quarters came down with a thud.

Unays whirled around when he heard that thud. He saw his animal sitting on the ground. "Rise!" he thundered. "Rise!" But the elephant did nothing. He just sat there swirling his great trunk lazily back and forth in front of him. Unays came running to him and snapped his whip across his hind end, but he didn't even seem to notice.

Abrahah jumped off his horse when he saw what was happening. He came running over to them.

"Ya Unays!! Make him get up! What kind of a trainer are you? You can't even make your own animal get up!"

This made Unays furious. He took an iron bar and beat the elephant on the head. When that didn't work, he poked his belly with an iron hook. But the animal didn't seem to feel anything. His sad, heavy eyes stared forward in their sacks of wrinkles and he chewed away at something inside his mouth.

Everyone was watching this and no one noticed Nufayl slip away, up into the hills to be with the Makkans.

Then they tried to trick the elephant. The first plan of attack was to follow the elephant to the Ka'ba. But when he wouldn't get up, Abrahah ordered his men to turn around and start moving in the other direction. Maybe the elephant would follow them!

It worked. The animal hoisted his grand hind end up into the air. Then he straightened first one front knee and then the other until he was standing. He started walking behind the soldiers. They all cheered. Then, by Abrahah's order, they all turned around and started walking towards him. He turned too, but when he found himself facing the Ka'ba again, he sat down. Nobody could make him get up. Allah says, "Be!" and it is, it surely is.

Some of the soldiers started whispering to each other. "It's a bad sign," said one. "We've never seen anything like this before."

Unays went to Abrahah. "Sir, something extraordinary is going on here! I've been with this elephant for thirty years and never ever have I seen him do anything like this! Let's turn back, until we know what is making him behave this way!"

"Preposterous!" bellowed Abrahah. "We've come this far, we are this close to destroying this place. I want my cathedral to be the place of pilgrimage for the whole world. Onward, I say! Onward to victory! Kill the foolish beast and leave it here to rot!"

Sweat was pouring down his face, and he was shaking. But he gathered up his reins, spurred his horse, and galloped off.

Ah, if only he had turned back then! All at once a dark wave washed across the sky from the direction of the sea. As far as they could see, the sky was filled with birds, spry little birds no bigger than sparrows, dark little birds flapping their wings and darting here and there like swifts. Each bird had a little pebble in its beak and one more in each claw, pebbles no bigger than dried peas. They dove and zinged down over the field and hurled their pebbles into the soldiers' bodies. No armour, no shield could help them against that rain. Their swords couldn't help them either.

The birds were screeching a cry that seemed to cut through the soldiers like knives right to their very bones. The men screamed and howled to block out that sound. They tried to run away, but there was nowhere to go. Their horses were neighing and prancing wildly. Their courage failed them. They screamed and twisted with pain. They begged for their lives, but there was nowhere to go, nowhere to hide, no way to escape the terrifying noise and darkness and fiery stones. Many of the soldiers were killed right away and their flesh began to rot there and then .

The birds slowly began to slip away. The darkness began to lift. A deep, terrifying silence fell over the dead, and over the wounded moaning soldiers who were still alive. The place looked like a wheat-field that had been razed by a terrible storm... not a single stalk of wheat left standing, the ground strewn with shredded leaves and stems.

A few of the wounded soldiers staggered off. Some of those died on the way home. Others, like Abrahah, got all the way home to the Yemen before they died, so that they would have to taste the bitterness of defeat for longer. The elephant and his trainer were not hit, not even with a single stone. They went back to the Yemen under clear blue skies.

The Ka'ba had not been touched. It stood, even as it stands today, gleaming and magnificent, a doorway to the Divine Mercy and Power of Allah, whose house it truly is.

The Quraysh of the Hollow, and their leader Abd al Muttalib, had relied on Allah and He had made them victorious. The way was open now for the completion of His message of Unity and Infinite Mercy and the birth of the Prophet Muhammad, may Allah bless him and give him peace. And many years later, after Muhammad, may Allah bless him and give him peace, was grown up and had become the Last Prophet, Allah recounted to him some of these happenings: